Seasons
of
Erotic Love

Barbara Herrera

Publishing Company

San Diego, California

Cover Design by Hummingbird Graphics
Book Design and Typesetting by Paradigm Publishing

Printed in the United States on acid free paper

Library of Congress Catalog Card Number: 92-061207
ISBN 0-9628595-4-0

Dedicated to all my ex-lovers — thanks
for the inspiration!

Table of Contents

Reading Erotica Aloud

Sharing thoughts, ideas, and feelings with other lesbians, as far as erotica is concerned, is vitally important to the sexual growth of our community.

Reading erotica aloud
Stimulates my Soul.
I feel everyone around me
Their auras crowd together.
Come with me!
Come together
to discover pleasure
Secrets exposed
Ideas whispered outside the sheets
FEEL what I say to you,
talk, Talk, TALK.
SHOUT!
Among yourselves.
What do you like?
This is what I like
do it . . . do me . . .
kiss here . . . touch there . . .
don't stop . . .

. . . talking!

Spring

Nourishment

Breasts, nipples, mouths, and tongues . . . what a delightful combination of sensations.

I suck from your breast
As if from life's source.
The softness oozes through my fingers
And I knead
(and I need!)
Making your nipple supple
With a hard knot of nipple
Tucked in my mouth
In between my teeth.
My tongue dances
Ancient memories
Trying to reclaim
What you do not have
Hidden inside there.
I can make you writhe and moan
Whilst I tug and pull,
Taste and nearly swallow,
Squish and massage,
Press and nearly scratch
You under my nails
Into my skin
Trying to consume you,
Impress upon you,
How much I love it
When
I suck from your breast.

Longings

Dreaming about being together heightens the tension, enough to last a lifetime.

You know, thinking about you touching me is so exciting! Not even just the sexual thoughts. The remembrances of your fingers reaching out to me, the way your hand feels on my waist, how it feels when I casually pass by you and all the others are near. Such small, benign gestures that evoke sparks—flashes of light, of love. Do you feel them, too? Seeing your hand on the table, I want to bring it to my lips. I want to kiss each fingertip; I want to lick every "V" in between your fingers. I want to take your wrist in my mouth and swirl my tongue around to make you quiver. I want my hair between, around, and through your fingers. I want to feel your hand pull my head back and I want to see your eyes gazing upon mine.

Feeling your hand on my waist, I want to feel your hand slide under my shirt. I want to feel my breast cupped in that hand. I want to feel your hand squeeze and release, squeeze and release—pumping adrenaline into my system. When I come near you, I want to turn, sit, look, kiss, touch, lick, taste, smell, feel, and hear you close to me. I want to lower myself to you and smell you as you sit and push your thighs apart. I want to pull your pants down and come close to you. I want you to sit and try to carry on a conversation with everyone while I separate your vulval lips and run my finger up one side, around your swelling clitoris, and down the other side. No one sees me and they wonder why you are gasping for air. You watch my face, my lips, my tongue come closer and reach out to you. Oooooooo—as I touch. Hot! You are so hot, and I love it. You've given up social graces and POOF everyone disappears.

You are alone with me and you tell me how good I feel, how much you've wanted me. I show you I've felt the same way for far too long. Your hand is on me, my hair through your fingers, just like I'd wanted it. I put one finger inside you, and when I pull out, I add another one. In. You are so wet. You are sloshing, soaking, and I try to keep up with you, my mouth full, my hand full.

Your head is back and I am so close to orgasm myself. I slow down—slow, slow, s l o w. My fingers stop moving. I want to feel your clit in my mouth. It is so soft, yet so hard. Your low growl lets me know you love it. I, too, love making love to you. You are so beautiful—the soft eyes, the hair with gold and white highlights, your breasts, your ass, your toes. I want to kiss them all. I wish I could cherish you the way I want to. With this pen, in my head, giving to you through my heart and words, I can show you. I can tell you how you feel to me.

I can feel you near me at times when it is impossible. Can you feel me touch you, taste you? Can you feel me in you? Can you feel me licking you, taking you in my mouth? Does your clitoris swell at times with no provocation? That is me! I am on you, in you, around you. Don't doubt Spirit Love—feel it! I make you come dozens of times every day. Sometimes, I even come with you.

I lick your clit; first with a hard tongue, then I soften. I relax my mouth and my tongue is flat, yet still going around stimulating all of you. You writhe, you moan. I lick. I've wanted to hear this for so long. I've wanted to feel you come for so long. Despite minimal stimulation, you are nearing climax. I decide it is time to show you.

I move my fingers in and out of your ever-tightening vagina. I turn my hand so the palm is facing the sky. Your juices are pooling there. I take my fingers and bend them, so I can feel your clitoris from the inside while kissing it on the outside. Pressure, pressure, pressure, while I quicken my pace. My tongue sweeps down to your opening and I push it in so that it may join my fingers, so it may taste your tartness. I move back up to your clit. My tongue knows where to move to make you come. I can *feel* it. I feel your vagina swell and tighten so my fingers can barely move; yet they don't stop. My tongue moves over your sensitive spot where I know you'll come. I only brush over it once every two or three times because I want to prolong this as long as possible. I hear you. Goddess, I hear you! You are begging me to make you come. It is all that I need to hear. Concentrate Energy. Love. Focus. Feel. Heat. Pressure. I feel you fill my mouth, squeeze my hand and you are there. You convulse, you hold me, you contract and relax, contract and relax. It is a hard one. My prolonging it worked! I wanted you to come hard. I slow while you catch your breath and I pull my mouth back but keep my hand moving. I can make you come again. You do. Afterwards, you want to kiss me so I slide (we are both so wet with woman and sweat) up to you and kiss you. Goddess, you taste wonderful. You tell me how much you want me and I let you make love to me. I come hard for you, too. Do you feel it? Do you feel me contract for you? Do you hear me scream for you?

I look in your eyes. I kiss your beautiful mouth. I touch your hair, your eyebrows, your nose, your lips. I touch your hand, your fingers. I snuggle in your arms, lay on your chest. I fall asleep feeling you running your fingers through my hair.

Secrets

Hidden love can be both fascinating and terrifying; a fact that makes it all the more exhilarating.

I sit next to you, feeling your leg next to mine. The energy between us buzzes, in secret, yet felt by others beside us. I feel you close and crave your touch. I imagine your hand brushing my shoulder. Your lips touch my neck and I feel your tongue lick my skin. I can't forget the chills I get every time you brush by me.

I want to kiss your lips when I'm near you. I want to feel your hand on my body. I have to stop my own from reaching out to touch your arm, your hair, your breast. I weigh what I can get away with in public or in private. I want to feel your tongue in my mouth, swirling around, making me so wet. I want to feel your hand on my breast, your fingers tugging, touching my nipple, making it so hard. I want to see you lower your mouth to my breast and pull my breast into your mouth. I feel my clitoris harden, as my nipple plays against the roof of your mouth. I reach out to touch your breast, too. It is already hard and I want you in my mouth. I can feel it.

I can feel it.

Your hand goes under me and you feel my heat. I shake while I anticipate your touch. I'm sitting in wet. Your fingers touch me and you moan, you are surprised by how slippery I am. How could you be surprised? I've imagined this moment hundreds of times. Haven't you? I feel you enter me and my vagina contracts around your fingers. I can feel every knuckle, every ridge. Your tongue going around and around my nipple feels almost like it's on my clitoris. Your fingers are going in and out. My juices are in the palm of your hand. The "O"s are escaping from my lips. I have no control over my vocal expressions. I have no control over my bodily expressions. Do you feel me shaking? Do you feel me wanting you?

You slide down my body and I feel your breath as cool, on my steaming, wet vulva. Your tongue reaches out tentatively and licks, slowly, slowly from bottom to top and I coat your tongue with me. I feel your lips surround my clitoris and your soft, wet, warm tongue rolls around and around my swollen—and growing more swollen with every revolution—clitoris. I ache to come. Your fingers inside me feel how tight I'm getting. Years of practice enable you to know exactly where to touch. And do you touch! I push love through my vulva to your mouth, your fingers, your hand, your body, your heart. I feel myself get huge and you ready yourself for my release. Arch, arch, arch—warmth, from my lower chakra, swirling around in circular motions, warmth spreading like ripples in a pond. My body is numb, yet all feeling. I know you can feel what I'm feeling, too, can't you? I explode into your mouth, into your soul, and you are there to catch me. I fall, shaking, shuddering into you and I feel you close, holding me.

Tears of joy and sadness slip from my eyes, and yours, and we treasure the moments we share. Holding on to each other, as we prepare to part and slip back into secrecy, yet again.

The Shroud

A woman makes love to an incest survivor and reflects on its inherent difficulties.

"Can I touch here?"

"Gently. Slowly, too."

It seems to get harder instead of easier sometimes to make love to Naomi. I love her so much, but one wrong move, or if the right move is too fast, my lover pulls away. Damn those fuckers who hurt the woman I love! I swear I'd kill them if they were sitting in front of me.

Instead, I have to be in the here and now so I can be hypersensitive to Naomi's needs. I wonder if we will ever be able to make love spontaneously and with wild abandon.

I touch her breast as if it might break off in my hand—a porcelain doll's fragility. I have to ask permission every step of the way.

"May I lick?"

"Yes."

So I do. I make slow, sensual motions, hoping to keep Naomi here with me. They were hard and cruel to her. If I'm gentle, maybe she'll forget them.

If only for a moment.

Her nipple responds to my tongue's play and hardens in my mouth. I want to touch her belly, so I lift up and ask if it's okay. She nods, so again I take her breast in my mouth and rub my hand over her belly. Naomi has such a soft belly. I like it so much. She's just learning to say "thank you" to compliments, so I offer them to her freely. She is such a beautiful woman. I love her hair, which she wishes could be tamed. Her deep green eyes, almost olive, belie the pain that lies right under the surface. She's so active in supporting other women's escapes and their own ensuing healing, I fear she forgets her own.

Tonight, she seems calm, so I enjoy letting my guard down just a bit. Her other breast beckons and I move, carefully, to the other side. My eyes implore and Naomi nods again. I want to swallow her nipple and have to relax so I don't get too rough. My hand moves lower on her belly and I lift up yet one more time: "May I make love to you, my darling Naomi?"

"Yes, Yael, please make love to me."

When she says this, I know I no longer have to ask to make each advance, but I say, "If you need me to stop, tell me." And she says, "Okay."

How many times we've had to stop because a fleeting, or stubborn, memory floated into her head. I hold her and love her and let her cry her pain away. I only wish it were that easy. The pain seems to spring anew, after working for weeks on a particular issue. Yet one more test to see if Naomi can let go. Always, two steps forward, one step back.

I slide down my lover's body and nestle between her legs. She smells so sweet and I tell her so. Here, where I am, is the hardest for her to handle. I tell her how brave she is to let me join her space, her close aura, and it comforts her. I kiss her thighs, lick them, and caress her outer thighs, while I hold them in my hands. I move closer to her vulva and talk to her while I nudge in.

"Oh, I love you. Your body is so beautiful. I love seeing how open you are. I love your beautiful woman parts . . ." My running dialogue lets her know that it is me—not them—and that I won't hurt her. I'm careful not to use the hate words as we call them; all the ugly words hurled at her during the abuse.

I start licking gently, touching her clitoris softly, and her body is responding positively. I feel her hips relax and she makes little sounds in her throat. I lick harder and begin swirling around her clitoris. Her pelvis begins its comfortable gyrations. When she stops, I know to stop, also. Tonight, though, she is full of enjoyment. Steadily, I circle her clitoris and I know she will orgasm soon. I love when she does, it's such a gift. For several months, Naomi would get just to the point of orgasm and stop. We both knew it was normal for that to happen, and yet it was still frustrating. It's rare when we have to stop so late in our lovemaking anymore. We've been told that each time we make love is an advancement in healing and we feel pleased, recognizing the progress.

Naomi releases herself to me in an act of absolute trust. I love her with all that I am and I know she feels it.

I heave my body up next to hers and ask her to lie on my chest so I may hold her. In my arms, she tells me how much she loves me, for my patience and for my love. I tell her she is worth any difference in how I used to make love. She says she is glad.

We lie in our embrace and I ponder why tonight so much thought is focused on her abuse. I think about the things I used to do with other women: penetration, vibrators, play-acting. I know Naomi isn't ready for any of that, she has told me so, and may not be for a long time—if ever.

But, I think even more fondly about how my lovemaking has changed for the better. I am slower, more focused, and certainly more considerate. I am able to detect nuances I hadn't noticed before. For those reasons, and hundreds more I could never verbalize, I am grateful for Naomi's presence in my life.

Not that frustrations, and even anger, never present themselves, but I am a gentler spirit, in all aspects of my life, for loving this incredible survivor.

Hot Dam!

Loving in the '90s can be complicated. Two women surpass restrictions as well as exceed all their expectations.

When the AIDS crisis began, I didn't pay much attention to it. Kim and I had been together nine years. Neither of us had had blood transfusions, nor had been with anyone in the high-risk categories. Neither one of us had been with anyone else at all. Ever. Period. We came out together.

Our sex, our wild, spontaneous sex, was fun. We'd touch each other anywhere we wanted to. We thought no one, and everyone, could see us. I made Kim have orgasms in those black-and-white photo booths you find every once in a while, in rides at amusement parks, and not always in the dark ones, and in the car more times than I can count. She always reciprocated and we never failed to derive great satisfaction from being so risque.

Our life together was fun at first, too. But we experienced so many changes as we grew older, that our relationship soon became a burden. Because we loved each other so much on one level and hated each other on another, we decided to call it quits.

I hurt for so long. I thought only of myself—how do I go on, how do I get to work, when do I feel like a human being again. When I realized that I was, indeed, going to make it and do okay, I started attending meetings at the Lesbian House. There, I listened to dozens of women tell stories so similar to mine, it was scary. I loved listening to them talk and laugh and cry. I loved seeing all those women feeling what I felt and still having hope that things would get better.

It was at about this time I started masturbating again. I wasn't sure I could handle the closeness of another woman yet, except in my fantasies. At first, Kim kept popping up in my mind. I'd find her in my arms and we'd be making love. After a couple of months of this, I started imagining I was making love to different women from group (I always chose a different one each week) and, just as my tongue would touch her clit, Kim would walk in and express her outrage. At first, I was shocked that she could pop up even without me thinking about her, but I soon ignored her and returned to whatever I was doing before she arrived. Finally, Kim disappeared from my mind and I could let go of her.

Getting to real flesh and blood women—now that was different. Not only was I scared about getting into another relationship, now I had to think about diseases: chlamydia, herpes, gonorrhea, syphilis, and, of course, the ultimate one—AIDS.

Now, I have to say, I'm a worrying kind of lesbian. I like to learn as much as I can before I do anything. I read the instructions on everything (even shampoo!). I checked out skiing books at the library before I learned to ski at Big Bear. So, it was no surprise that I would want to learn all I could before having sex with someone else.

Don't laugh. I went to seven "Safe Sex for Lesbians" workshops even before kissing another woman. For me, the changes that had happened in nine years were scary. I wanted to be *sure* I was taking care of myself. Honestly, I went to all seven workshops to be certain I got all the information that was available. One never knows when someone might forget a small, yet vital, piece of information. I admit that all the speakers said about the same thing. Most of them were funny, but one just droned on. I know AIDS is serious business, but sex is supposed to be fun!

After I lost my embarrassment about being there, about meeting number three, I got into the stuff we were being taught. It was nice putting dental dams on our hands and licking to see if I could really feel my tongue through the rubber. I was as surprised as everyone else that I could, in fact, feel quite well through the dam! We layered finger cots, pretending clitoral stimulation was what we had in mind, or wore a couple of pairs or more of latex gloves as we mentally readied ourselves for penetration.

Silly as we sometimes got, tasting the different flavored items or imagining scenarios when we'd actually *use* this knowledge, we all knew the importance of the information.

So, amid our embarrassment, we listened intently and learned.

I have to admit that I wondered, along with many others, whether sex would be as good while practicing safe sex. Would I ever find that wild abandon again? I was soon destined to find out.

Malina and I went from group-mates, to friends, to romantic interests. Because we went to group together, she knew I didn't sleep around and that I laid out rules before I would go to bed with any woman. I told everyone, quite haughtily, now that I think about it, that I would have safe sex and that we both would have HIV tests at the beginning of the relationship, at three months, and at six months even before I would think about having unprotected sex. I got stares and laughs until I said that I loved myself enough to keep myself alive, and whoever I was with would have to respect that. After a terribly uncomfortable amount of time, a voice in the corner said, "Good for you." The subject moved on to self-love, so I was left alone with my decision.

Malina was holding my hands and staring into my eyes and I could feel my thighs on fire. Now, as much of a worrier as I am, I am also really into sex. All this safe-sex stuff seemed to be a total pain in the ass sometimes—but only until the next new report said that women get AIDS much easier than men, or that a cure is still years away.

I leaned over and gave her a sweet kiss on the cheek. She lowered her dark eyes and smiled shyly. I asked her what do we do now and her answer still amazes me. She said, "We have our blood tested, because I want to be able to show you how much I love you." I pulled her to me and buried my face in her coat. I remember the smell of her hair, her sweat under her coverings, the way her scarf scratched my cheek with its wooliness.

And so we finally find ourselves together in bed. Malina's sweetness wafts into my being. This is our first time, but it is more comfortable than I imagined it would be. My soon-to-be lover says she feels the same way.

Our goodies are in a velvet-lined basket, and after we undress each other, we explore what's inside.

I pull out lube, finger cots in assorted colors, different size gloves—all unpowdered—and dozens of dental dams.

Both Malina and I have shared our fears and hopes during the past two weeks and here we are—doing what I said I'd do.

In the background, Therese Schroeder-Sheker plucks her harp for us and I choose a purple finger cot for my forefinger, and slide it on. There's a blue one for my middle finger, pink for my ring finger, and bright green for my pinkie. My thumb needs one, too, so I pull a pastel yellow onto it and my fingers dance in the candlelight. Malina laughs and says, "Let your fingers do the walkin'," and lies back, enticing me with her own hands that stroke up and down her belly while I apply lube to my rainbow of latex fingers.

I lean over her and kiss her forehead, my nipple falling into her mouth. Malina draws it in and I shudder with anticipation. I kiss her cheeks and her nose, and Malina loses my breast. I move to kiss hers and run my tongue up and down over her breast, making it stand up on end. I take the tip between my teeth and pull back. My lover groans her pleasure and I sink forward, sucking in as much as I can to fill my mouth. She tastes incredible. The softness is wonderful, the contrasting hardness of her nub sends shivers right to my clit.

My colored fingers slide down her belly and search for her other, more sensitive nub. I keep licking her nipple, and her whole breast, as I find her clitoris hidden between her swollen labial lips. I bend my violet finger and tickle her clit—tease it to arousal. It takes some moments before I can grasp it between my thumb and forefinger, but when I do, I massage the opposite sides of her clit at the same time. I hear her woman's moans getting louder, so I release her nipple and slide down the bed farther. I position myself between her legs and smell her heavy, musky scent. I now see her clit, it glows its redness at me. I can almost feel the heat it gives off.

I concentrate on her nodule and use my purple digit to stimulate it. My hand stays in the same position, palm down, and I move my hand so that her clit goes around and around the tip of my finger. Her energy zips up my hand and I feel my nipples harden under me. Her clit gets bigger and bigger and my revolutions accelerate.

I stop.

I take the soft padded tip of my finger and stroke, quickly, up and down, flicking as a tongue would.

Malina arches and I watch her hands pull at the sheets. She holds her breath . . . and then lets out the noises of release, while I watch the entrance to her vagina contract and relax—begging me to come inside.

I fumble for the basket and pull out a pair of gloves. While I put them on, I tell Malina I'm going to enter her cavern. I tell her I can't wait to hear her swishing, wet noises. I grab another pair of gloves and put them over the first, which went over the finger cots, too. My right hand is decorated with faint colors showing through the yellowish tinted, lubed latex.

I look up and Malina is staring at me in a daze. I ask her if she's okay, does she still want me? She comes back into herself and tells me she wants me bad, she just was dazed from the excitement. I sigh with relief and ask her if she is ready now. She tosses her head back into the pillow, spreads her legs, and says, "I'm ready."

I put my left hand over her right thigh on the bed and hold myself up, while I move my right hand to feel Malina's pubic hair, her lips, and her clit. The heat I thought I felt before exists and I am about to be swallowed up in it. I slowly push my forefinger in and I hear her moan with pleasure. I use another finger and enter her—she repeats the sound, but louder and deeper this time. I add a third finger and then a fourth; each time Malina's vocalizations become less inhibited.

Her noise, her wetness, her heat excites me and I feel my clit reaching out to touch hers.

I start slowly and gradually quicken my strokes. My thumb, barely perceptible, brushes against her clit. I hear her tell me "harder" and I oblige. In and out, in and out. The sticky sounds I hear make me hungry for the hard nub in front of my thumb. I push in harder. She has let go so much, her legs are bent and her knees are almost touching the bed. She's so open for me. She's so open to me. I get up on my knees and lay my head on her belly. Like this I can move my arm fast without much strain. Malina's vagina is tightening on my fingers. She's going to come. Her commands of "harder" have changed to "Yes!" and I push with everything I have. Malina screams out a long, singular "YES!" as I keep up my frantic pace, so I can outdistance her pulsating vagina.

As she slows down, I do, and when she relaxes, I exit her cavern as slowly as I entered it.

I look down at my hand and it is covered with the white cream of the woman I love.

I see her clit still peeking out and tell Malina the best is yet to come. She sighs, and laughs, and asks how it could possibly get any better. I tell her to relax and I will show her.

I carefully remove the gloves by pulling the top down over the wet without touching it. This causes the gloves to turn inside out, and as long as they are thrown away immediately, which I do, the wet stays inside. When I get to the fingers of my gloves, I lift the finger cots off in a similar manner and they come off inside the gloves.

I pull a fresh pair from the basket and put them on each hand. I talk with Malina about what she's feeling and she tells me she's feeling so good, so content. I ask her if she is still aroused and her dark curls scatter on the pillow as she nods her head up and down.

I look in the basket and carefully choose what I want. I tell Malina to spread her thighs again for me and I lower myself onto the bed. I take the blood red dental dam, spread it between my gloved fingers, and lay it on her vulva. I'm glad I thought to include a variety of colors because, as I gape at her swollen clitoris, red is the only color I can imagine licking; the burning color that only comes from inside a woman. I remember that the scarlet latex is cherry-flavored and I know that I am going to enjoy myself.

Aiming for her clit underneath its covering, I lick. Her noises tell me this really works, she feels me despite the barrier! This thrills me and I commence my tongue dance on her hard button.

When we were planning our evening, we talked about buying one of the garter-belts that held dental dams in place. They were new but I wasn't sure how comfortable we would be wearing one. Would we each need our own because we're such different sizes? What if it snapped, or let go? I talked to several women who said they thought they were great, it gave them their hands back. Others said they didn't like them at all. I wasn't sure what to do. Malina suggested we do without it for a while and see how it goes. I told her I thought that was a great idea.

My hands hold the latex and touch her thighs. The cherry flavor is wearing off, but Malina's excitement is feeding me now, so I don't care. I can feel her clit swelling and press harder to urge her on. My tongue goes back and forth, up and down, around and around—and Malina stops breathing, arches (and I keep up with her), and she comes as I let go of the soaked dental dam and push three fingers into her dripping hole. Quickly, I rise up to lean over her and guide my hand in and out in even rhythms to coax yet another orgasm out of my lover.

I am rewarded, and she is also, as she comes yet again.

Her breathing is fast and hard—a mirror image of how I make love to her.

Oh, it's my turn to feel her hands all over me. I get to experience her hand deep inside, her tongue licking me to a raging climax.

Yes, it's my turn.

Summer

Peaches

As this story demonstrates, eating a Georgia peach can be a sensual experience.

Reading this aloud, or to yourself, with a slow, Southern drawl heightens the experience and the pleasure eating peaches affords.

I've known times when I'd have driven to Atlanta or Augusta or Statesborough in muggy June just for a Georgia peach.

Finding just the right tree along a country road, I'd stand under it, looking up. Seeing the peaches hanging heavily on their limbs, I would reach up, as I do to my lover's breast when she's standing above me, and caress the softness, the warmth of its velvety girth.

Pulling the fruit to me, hearing the gentle snap as it falls into my hands, I bring it to my face and smell the hot sweetness while I rub it against my cheek. This peach is weighty; red over most of her skin and oversized in my hand. If I press too deeply, she bruises, so I pour water from the jug over her and wash her gently. Feeling all of her softness and praising the Goddess as I baptize this fruit for my consumption.

Sweat drips off my brow and mingles with the water. My mouth salivates as I anticipate the bite into my sun-warmed gift. I raise the peach to my mouth, inhale deeply, and sink my teeth into the soft flesh. Juice dribbles down my chin, hot and sticky, and I'm covered with golden liquid up to my elbows. My hand turns the peach so I may continue my feast while my tongue feels the incredible smoothness on the underside of the skin. If it were cold outside, steam would rise from the heat trapped near the fruit's core, but it is hot, making the meat even hotter.

Each bite, luscious and sensuous, brings my own wetness to the surface. I lick slowly, imprinting each ridge, each millimeter, into my brain. This may be the only peach I will ever eat, so I will make it last. I want to rub the peach, oozing juice, all over me and mix it with my sweat, my own hidden secretions, yet I continue eating. Biting gently, rolling each section in my mouth, feeling it. Then chewing—c h e w i n g. I can almost feel each capsule of fluid *burst* as my teeth and tongue devour the fruit.

I've known times when I'd have driven to Atlanta or

Augusta or Statesborough in muggy June for a Georgia peach, but I've been too far away to do it. So I find just the right woman along the road in my life, I stand under her, caress the softness, smell her hot sweetness, and then . . . sink my teeth in.

So Far Away . . .

Night time is lonely until visions invade the mind . . .
and the soul.

It is past midnight. It's a hot, muggy, sweaty night. I've tossed and turned for over an hour. I lay in bed reading until 11:00, masturbated (making wonderful love to you, did you feel me?) and turned the lights out. Thoughts of you flow in and out of my mind. Where are you in your dream state? Does insomnia attack you, too?

I keep *feeling* you. You are so, so soft—as a woman should be. I press my fingers in your arm and become one with you for a moment. I can smell you, so sweet. My lips graze your neck until I find the place I've waited for—the place I've dreamed about for centuries. Then my lips are stranded, hesitate, then lower to your flesh. I want to taste you, yet I'm afraid of scaring you away. I want to mesmerize—hypnotize you—but perhaps not quite yet. Will the time ever be right?

But in my dream, I continue . . .

I lick your softness. The slow-motionness that happens is in full effect. I lick and taste your salt. I feel the flesh rise beneath my tongue; you shudder. I can kiss your neck, from front to back to front again, hundreds of times. And so I do.

I feel your lips with my fingertips. I kiss each crease and lick, making your lips as moist as mine have been. I feel each ridge of each tooth with my tongue and I slide my tongue toward yours.

So warm, so very warm. Your body, your aura, your arms, your lips, your tongue—your love. So very warm. My hands begin to feel your body. So soft.

You are feeling me—
Feeling me touch your shoulders—
and kiss them.
I touch your arm—
and kiss.
With every inch of you I feel—
I kiss.
I can *see* you. I can *feel* you. How can this be, when I

have never been next to you for more than a few hours? How many lives have we shared? Surely more than this one.

I can feel your breast in my hand, your nipple swelling in my mouth. I can hear your breath become labored while my mind caresses your soul. I can't touch your body in all the places I want in unison, so I see them, and it is your turn to feel me. You shake, tremble, sigh, shudder while I envelope you with me. I feel your breast, your hip, your navel, your thigh, your clitoris, your neck, your toes, your wrist, in my mouth, on my tongue. And I'm going 'round and 'round and 'round. I will make the sign for infinity through every pore on your body. I will remind your woman-self why she is lesbian with lesbian circles all over you. I will feel you sweat, pulse, and swell within my mouth. I will swallow you, inhale you, ravish you—yet still remain starved.

For every time you release your soul to me and give me all of you, I will praise the Infinite Universe for putting you in my tapestry.

Dimensions

Loving, and making love to, voluminous women evokes powers and strengths many women do not have, whether it is because of adversities overcome or because of the sheer magnitude of their presence.

Her touch was driving me crazy. I wanted her fingers on me, in me. I couldn't get enough of her. Her flesh squishes under my fingers and I squeeze hard enough for her to know I am responding positively to her overtures. Goddess, I love making love with a fat woman! She is so *there*. Her space is so defined and I have to ask her if I can share her space. She makes no apologies about the amount of personal space she utilizes or that she likes to sit on two chairs instead of one. I learned early to patronize places that had no arms on their chairs and had bathrooms she could turn around in. I never noticed the oppression fat women face. What a stupid society that rejects and ignores fat women like the one I love.

We finally drove into our driveway and I couldn't get into the apartment soon enough. She pressed me up against the wall and surrounded me with her Self. "Fuck me, Hill. I want it bad." We dropped the bags of groceries and Hillary undid the buttons on my jeans. Still leaning against the door, she slid her hand down my belly and into my underwear to touch my wet. She had to wriggle for a moment so she had a good angle, but then she took one finger and moved it back and forth to spread my lips. I slumped over her shoulder, hardly able to contain my grunts and groans. Always wary of the neighbors who insist on banging on the wall in the throes of my passion, I bury my face in her neck. Hillary took one finger and pushed it deep into my puss. "Oh, Leya, you are so wet. It's so hot in here." I could feel my clit against her finger and her finger deep inside me. We had been talking dirty to each other the whole time we were at the store so I was ready to come in her hand. Hill plunged her hand in and out of me and I began the early contractions of orgasm. I could have waited longer except her hand was putting so much pressure on my vulva and her finger was rubbing directly on my clit. I sank my teeth into her neck and exploded my release of all that anticipation. Hillary held me tight and let me shrink into her arms.

I wanted to make love to her so we put the groceries away and now we are taking a candlelit shower together. I love being in here with her. It's so hot and steamy, I always feel like I'm in a movie when I take a shower with someone. Movie sets couldn't be this warm and romantic, though.

Hillary disrobes and stands before me naked and open. I can't see her pubic hair, but I know it is there because I play with it when we are lying in bed. Her hair is sparse because of the ample flesh and I love licking between each of the hairs, tickling her into arousal.

Both of us get into the shower and I watch her lean her head back and get wet. I take the soap and run it down her body, touching, feeling, craving her body. I hold her left breast in my hand and savor the weight of it. Her nipple is the size of the palm of my hand, and once again, I apologize to her for not being able to please her by taking all of it in my mouth. She looks up, then down, and tells me I please her better than any of her previous lovers and to quit it. I tell her I bet she says that to all her lovers. She says, "Yes, as a matter of fact I have said that to all my lovers." She doesn't say this to be mean, but it still bites a little. "I know more about myself and about my body with each lover, so I suppose that is why I say that. Does that make sense?" I tell her she makes perfect sense and I am so glad she was there to tell me how to please her because she deserves it. Hillary touches the small of my back and pulls me close. "You, too, deserve the best. Tell me where to touch you, my darling Leya." I turn around and encourage Hillary with the gyrations of my ass. She takes the soap and fills her hands with suds. Bending down, she washes me. Her hands slide around my ass, my puss, cleaning me for later. Hillary's two fingers move up and down with my clit in between them. I feel the heat so acutely now that I'm flushed. I know my clit must be sliding in and out of her hood. I feel the streams of water hitting my clit at even intervals. Holding on to the soap dish to avoid falling down, I come once again in

Hillary's hand.

I sit on the floor of the bathtub to collect myself and ask Hill to turn the water on cold for a minute. I feel refreshed and turned on by the sudden change in temperature and tell Hillary I want her puss in my mouth. She laughs and tells me I'll just have to wait because the shower isn't big enough for her to spread her thighs far enough apart to fit my face in there. It is big enough for her to take her puss in her hand and show me her clit and how big it is. I lunge for it and she reminds me she can't come standing up. I tell her I don't care and proceed to part her lips so I can go inside her and feel her heat. Oh! The contrast between the cold shower and the heat of her puss is incredible! How does she get so hot? Every time I enter her I am surprised by the intensity of her passion. Even after four years, I shudder each time I squish inside her and make noises in her puddles. Hill contracts as I go deep inside her vagina and I lose all of my hand and much of my arm between her thighs. The pressure is intense for both of us as I wiggle my finger around inside her without moving my hand. She loosens up and I put another finger in. It's always easier for me to move two fingers at the same time, I have great rhythm that way. I swirl my digits in unison and touch what I call her shelf (what the het people named the "G" Spot). If I were looking at my hand, my pointer and middle finger would be bent almost to the palm of my hand. That is what I do inside my lover. It drives her crazy. Pressure, release, pressure, release. Hillary moans her pleasure and I see her knees buckling. That is my signal to stop, so I turn the water off and we get out of the shower.

I watch Hillary walk to the bed and her body is in motion. Every part of her moves: thighs, breasts, arms, calves, and her ass. Oh, her ass . . . I wish I had enough hands to hold her whole butt at one time. Instead, I ask her to lie down on her stomach so I can massage her. She looks delighted and complies. I grab the lotion and dash to the bed. Hillary's face is buried in the pillows and I squirt lotion on my hands to warm it before rubbing it on her body. Mmmm, I touch the warmed liquid to her body and her dimples and crevices with my fingers. As I touch, and honor, this gigantic presence, I remember Hillary telling me of the humiliation and embarrassment she had growing up in the heterosexual, "You can never be too rich or too thin" culture. She told me she spent years trying to conform to standards she was never meant to meet. I remember her face looking sad and without color as she tapped into this memory. But her face re-lit when she spoke of the joy and happiness she experienced on the discovery of Self Love; not only through her acknowledged sexuality, but also in her heart for who she is, not for what she looked like. Never before having had a lover over two hundred pounds, it was quite a shock to find myself crazy in love with a woman well over three hundred pounds. Some people questioned my motives, "You just want to see what she looks like naked, don't you?" Some women couldn't believe I really was sexually attracted to her, "Don't you think she should lose weight? She is awfully big." Still others couldn't imagine what I would do with her when I got to make love to her, "What will you do with all that woman?" For all the women who passed Hillary by, for all the women who made fun of her because of her size, and for all the women who are blind to beauty because of our social indoctrination—too fucking bad for you! You have lost out and I have won the heart of a woman I will never leave and will always love, no matter what size she is now, or in the future.

"OW!"

"Oh, baby. I'm sorry. I didn't mean to pinch so hard." My anger must have made me massage a bit too vigorously. I relax and think about love and flowers and sex and peace while I breathe the yucky stuff out and the good stuff in. Hillary relaxes also, and I start massaging the insides of her thighs. I take a pillow and ask her to move one leg up onto the pillow so I can reach her puss. I can see its wet darkness now and start feeling closer and closer to it. I excuse myself for a moment and quickly wash my hands so nothing will get into her gorgeous puss. When I come back, I spread her lips apart with my fingers and hear the wet. My clit is getting so hard. Fucking her backwards takes some deftness—everything is upside down—so I don't worry about the shelf, I just give her some good hard strokes. Usually, I take my other hand and press it into her vulva so she has pressure on her clit. This time, I want to eat her so bad, I ask her to turn over. She does, and I swoon at her massive breasts lying before me. I put my finger back in her and lie beside her so I can suck her nipples at the same time.

I always make myself crazy with what to do first, middle, and last. So many places to pleasure her, and myself, and every time I ask her, she says, "Everywhere." Some help, huh? Her nipple is swelling in my mouth and I feel the outer ridges bumping the outside of my upper and lower lips. She is moaning and moving her hips in rhythm to my fingers while I suck harder and harder, flicking her nipple with my tongue. Sucking noises escape my mouth when I lose contact with her breast, but I just suck more frantically and I get it again.

Hill is heavy in her ecstasy and I realize I have yet to eat her. I ask, gasping for air, if I can, please, eat her. She slows her hips and tells me, "Eat me now. I want to come in your face." A shiver of pleasure runs through me and my hand gently leaves her pussy. I prop Hillary up on pillows so she can watch me. When she lies flat, she can't see me because her belly is there. I love looking up and seeing her face gazing down at me, eyes intense, mouth open and wet. When she is ready, I push her thighs apart and inhale deeply, intoxicating myself with her scent. Her vulval lips are full and swollen. They call me with their own hunger, so I suck on her left lip and slide my tongue on the inside, getting a hint of the juices available so close to my mouth. I put my hands around her thighs and hold on for the ride ahead of us both. I turn my head and suck on her right lip. Pulling back, I notice her wet is dripping down to the crevice in her ass, so I put my tongue there and slowly lick bottom to top, piling her nectar on my tongue. When I reach the apex, I swallow a mouthful of sweet, sticky love and begin shaking in anticipation of Hillary's orgasm. My tongue finds its way into her cavern and I tongue-fuck her and swallow in even intervals of enjoyment. Hill starts to writhe and I hold on to her legs. A small orgasm, with a big gush of liquid, tells me it is time to move to the more sensitive part of her vulva: her clitoris. I slide my tongue up and pull my right hand from under her leg at the same time. Her clit has become engorged and I will feed off it until she is spent. My tongue knows the motions, *feels* where she wants me to lick. My eyes are closed and my face is buried in her puss. My own wet flows unchecked as I eat from my lover and visualize Hillary's pleasure while offering her more. Around and around and around her clit, moving in a design lesbians have known since the beginning of time. Lightly now, making my breath have more weight than my tongue. Hot air, hotter puss, pull back, blow lightly, cold air, tight lips, make the air blow in a chilly circle around her clit. I glance up and see her nipples harden from the icy stream I've given her down here. My left hand reaches up and touches her pebble-hard nipple. I decide to keep it in my hand and play with it while I feast from her vagina. I wrap my lips around her clit and make my tongue very soft and flat. I have continual pressure on her clitoris, but a perception of revolutions is there, too. I figure this will drive her close to orgasm, but I will still have control over when she comes. All I need to do is release pressure and she will move farther from her climax. If I feel she is not as close as I want her to be, I press harder. All the while my tongue is moving around, and as it sweeps over the top of her hood, she feels chills of pleasure. I hit that spot every second or so, just long enough for the feeling to subside before I'm on it again. It drives her wild. My right hand edges up to the opening and relaxes, knowing what comes next. I continue playing with her nipple and licking at her puss, but now I will enter her wet and fuck her as well. I push my finger in tentatively, and with every inward motion, my finger advances farther. When I cannot push in any longer, I pull out a little and add a finger. I repeat the sequence and hear Hillary moan with each advancement. A mantra of "Yes . . . yes . . . yes . . ." flows from her lips. I add yet a third finger into Hillary; my hands seem small tonight. Perhaps it is Hillary's excitement that has made her so open. I know that soon, I will have my hands squished because of her contractions around them. I don't mind and I start my acceleration to get to that end. Hillary is moving her hips to my constant in and out, around and around, and pull and tug. Low growls tell me how much pleasure she is feeling and I begin to groan, too. The vibrations affect her deeply; she nears her climax and I gush juice from my own puss. I love feeling how big her clit gets in my mouth. Her vagina tightens around my hand, pulling me in, in, in . . .

I picture myself tumbling head-first into my lady's cavern. Looking around, do I see ridges of deep, red creases? No, more like folds, pleats. As her excitement increases, her insides stretch and her puss becomes a long tunnel. I wander around exploring, getting closer to her purple cervix. When I fuck her, I hit it every once in a while. Sometimes she says it hurts and other times she says, "harder." I'm standing at the back of her vagina admiring her cervix. The whole thing looks like a swollen donut, her *os* (the opening into her uterus) is pressed almost closed—she's a long way from either ovulation or her period. I move backwards and feel the sticky wet around me, turn around and see her glands oozing liquid. I want to lick it, so I run toward the outside so I can get back into my body. As I exit her puss, I look up and see her clit. I can't leave without paying homage to it, so I climb up her inner lips and gasp at the power, gape at the enormity of her swollen clitoris. An aura of ecstasy revolves around her exposed nerve center. I stroke it and am in awe of its velvety softness, its slippery dew, and its retracting hood. Seeing her clit raw with feeling, I put my face to it and am dwarfed by the size. I close my eyes and I feel her pressed into my face; I open them and her clit is huge in my mouth, between my lips.

Hillary is close to orgasm and I fuck her hard while I suck from her wet. Her body writhes in time to my strokes inside her and my circles around her clit. I feel my body anticipating her orgasm and tiny contractions spring forth from my uterus. Goddess, we are both so wet! I give Hillary my energy via her clit and I send her through the roof. I feel her arch in expectation and hold on so I can keep up all the stimulation. Stopping now would end her build up and I want her to come hard. Her vagina contracts around my fingers and I can barely move my hand, so I move my fingers on her shelf. I can feel her clit from behind when I do this, so I lick and press from both sides at the same time. This sends Hill into her last frenzy and she gets still tighter and her clitoris swells until I think it will explode—and it does! My mouth is blessed with her clit shoving energy down my throat. My hand holds something more tangible: juices, wet beyond belief! And I feel her squeeze my fingers in her puss until they can no longer move. I have never felt a woman come for as long as Hillary and it surprises me every time. She continues her pulsations for a minute or so after her initial orgasm. I stay with her while she is in such a heightened state of enjoyment. She pushes my head away from her clit, but lets my hand continue to plunge in and out of her. I feel another orgasm coming on the heels of the one she just had and I fuck her hard so she can come again without losing the sensation of the one before. Her pussy contracts yet again and I hear her come as she grunts out her pleasure. I love hearing her moan to the contractions, her body in perfect synchronization.

Hillary pulls me up to her and I gently remove my soggy hand. I move up to her and revel in her softness. I lay on her left side, my head on her heaving chest, my arm around her waist, and my leg thrown over hers. "I love you," I say. When she catches her breath, she says, "I love you, too, baby." She starts rubbing me absently as she composes herself and I know I am next. I get shivers as I picture her between my thighs, her hot tongue on my warm clit, her fat fingers inside my tight puss, the weight of her body on top of mine as she fucks me hard while I fuck her, and my own orgasm exploding in her face and on her body . . . yes, I know that is what's coming next.

But that's another story . . .

Time to Play

Finding the time to make love with small children underfoot sometimes requires wizardry, but when it happens, magic ensues.

Do you know what a luxury time is when we make love?
Do you realize the magic it takes to make three, though
usually four or five, pre-schoolers disappear?

Ah, but when it happens . . .

I'll hold you close to me for our few precious hours alone
as soon as the door closes and the kids go hopping and
screeching down the hall. I'll look into your eyes and will
not worry about a child clamoring at my leg for attention—my
attention is on you. I can now focus my Energy on you. I
won't hear someone in the background yell "Mom-
mmmyyy!" as I put my fingers inside you (as has happened
so many times before). I'll touch your face and kiss your
cheeks. Mmmm, the smell of you on your neck.

A kiss, light, sweet . . .

Shit! That damn phone. "I know, I am . . ." Turn it
down, turn the answering machine down, too. "No baby, I
promise, no more interruptions."

Where were we? Kissing?

Yes, kissing. Soft, sweet kisses. Already I can feel myself
ready for loving you. Your tongue is so warm, your breath,
too, as we part to take a moment for air. "Can we take a
shower together? A long, hot one (another treat when the
kids are gone; sharing the bathroom with the person of your
choice!)." I take your clothes off and marvel at your body as
I unveil it. Why do we have to wear clothes at all? Your
breasts in my hands . . . more warming softness. I undress
myself while you wait impatiently for the water to get hot
enough. Don't you know it'll be so hot in this tiny room
that we'll feel lightheaded later? "Take my hand. I'll help
you in."

Belly to belly, you feel so good next to me. I hold you
while you slowly roll your head back to wet your hair. The
water bounces off of you and it's cold when it hits me—it
makes my nipples hard—but that's okay, your hands on
them do that, too. I get the shampoo and squirt some in my
hands. I have to turn and face the shower spray, your ass is

to my puss, and oh does it feel good!

I know. I'm washing your hair . . .

My hands on your head rub and scrub and twist your short hair into comical shapes. I giggle at you and you want to see what you look like, but I slide my hand over my creation to erase it. In revolt, you step under the streaming water. So, I touch your breasts again, this time with meaning. I lower my mouth to your nipple and I pull it in. I love how it fills my mouth, the nipple against the roof of my mouth. One hand is around your waist and one is filled with you. The hand around your waist falls lower to feel the soft curves of your butt and I move to kiss your belly, its folds and its evidence of life experiences. The water's getting in the way, so I turn you around. Now I'm getting drowned by the water's deluge on my face. I get the soap and begin cleaning you for my personal worship service. From head to toe, literally, washing behind your ears with the washcloth, in between your fingers and toes, under your arms, and, carefully, the folds of your vulva. I put you frontwards to wash all the soap off and scratch your back. You coo as I cover your back with red marks. I'm so hot from the water—and the want—and my hands are pruny. You say it's okay to let me wash myself quickly so we can get out of the heat. Wet, we open the bathroom door and steam flows out as the cool air comes rushing in. You dry me and then dry yourself. We race to the bed and jump under the covers. I snuggle into your arms and hold you tightly. You do the same to me. Slight kisses sprinkle your chest as I roll toward you. My tongue tastes your freshly scrubbed self and my hands explore parts of you not yet accessible to my mouth. Rising up, I kiss you deeply and whisper loving secrets only shared between us. I invite you to be my altar and you mumble something like, "Yes, baby, do anything you want."

So I do.

I enter your temple and am absorbed in the heat, the

wet, the smells. I taste you and praise the Goddess for making women. I languish in your softness and feel parts of you quiver—parts deep within.

Time stands still, yet speeds ahead. Do I hear the kids? No! A quick glance at the clock shows hours still to go. Thank you, I pray! I am feeling what you are feeling. I *love* what you're feeling. My tongue circles your clitoris and it's so delicious I want to roll it around in my mouth for a while. I put my fingers inside you to feel what it feels like from the inside. Wet. WET. And getting so tight hugging my hand. My tongue is following your lead and we're so high, so far away. I can feel your orgasm getting closer and give you love—from tongue to clitoris—as you start to emit glitter from your inner world. I slow down to prolong the other-dimensional feeling. I feel you slipping between two places and choose to lose you for a moment, to give you a well-deserved vacation. Your glitter looks like stars in my face as they explode from your vulva. Your vagina contracts and relaxes a dozen times before I feel you coming back to our bed. I come to kiss you, and thank you, with you still fresh on my mouth. I submit to your expressions of love and have a glorious time. After our reciprocal exchanges, we collapse for a few minutes before we pull ourselves together for our kids' return.

Making dinner, tying shoes, giving baths, reading goodnight stories—all the mundane habits will feel fresh tonight because of you. I close my eyes amidst the chaos . . . see you sparkle . . .

. . . and life goes on . . .

Over the Line

Phone sex is safe sex. Or is it?

"Hello?"

"It's me."

"Oh."

"I'm naked."

"Oh?"

"I'm sitting on the bed."

"Uh huh . . ."

"I've got the phone cord between my legs."

"Sounds delightful!"

"My nipples are hard."

"Even better. May I come over?"

"No. I want to tell you what I'm doing. Stay there."

"Okay."

"I feel the cord next to my clit and I'm pulling it up and down."

"The cord or your clit?"

"Both."

"Oh."

"I bet I'm wet."

"Feel."

"Yup. I'm wet."

"Feel deeper."

"Mmmmm . . ."

"What?"

"It's hot as hell in there. My finger is covered with my wet."

"Suck it."

"Mmmmm . . . sweet today."

"May I come over?"

"No!"

"Why not?"

"I want to tease you."

"You are!"

"Good."

"Wanna shower with me?"

"Bitch."

"C'mon, it could be fun."

"I *know* it would be fun. Won't you electrocute yourself?"

"I didn't say a shower, I said a shower massage, but I'll use the cordless phone, just in case."

"Okay, but I'd really like to watch."

"Tough. Oh my, you should see the phone cord."

"I'd like to."

"Wait, let me switch phones."

"You there?"

"Of course! You think I'd leave? It's just getting good."

"Let me get the water warm. What are you doing now?"

"While you switched phones I got naked, too. I don't have the luxury of a shower massage or a cordless phone so I guess I'll just have to suffer with my own hand."

"Poor baby. Water's warm."

"Are you in?"

"Yup."

"What'cha doin'?"

"Sitting on the bottom."

"Where's the shower massage?"

"In my hand."

"Where's it pointing?"

"Guess."

"Your pudendum?"

"My what?"

"Pudendum. It's a scientific word. Latin for . . ."

"Cunt?"

"Nicer."

"Crotch?"

"More sensual."

"Cavern?"

"Ah . . . cavern . . . that's better. A deep, dark, secret, oozing place."

"Sounds yummy."

"I'm sure you are. Where's that water?"

"We just went through that, didn't we?"

"My finger is on my clit."

"Oh yeah? What's it doing?"

"Going around it. Sliding over it. Slipping down to pick up more juices and bring them back up."

"Mmmm . . . I feel the water doing what your finger is doing."

"Describe it."

"Let's see . . . I feel lips on the outer edges of my vulva—a constant pressure there. Then I feel a dancing sensation above my clit."

"I feel pressure on mine as I move my finger around it. It excites me to hear what you are doing."

"Good. Wanna hear more?"

"Yes."

"I'm holding the phone on my shoulder so I can reach down and spread my lips apart. The water's beating on the inside—god is it getting intense."

"I hear that! I'll put more pressure on mine so I can keep up. Can I tell you what I see?"

"Please."

"I see your mouth all wet and hungry. I see you pulling my jeans down and finding my G-string panties you like so much, the ones that crawl up my ass. I turn you on so you shove my tee shirt up and you see that I've decorated the top of me, too, with my half bra, the pink and black lace one. Your tongue licks my nipples, sucks them in your mouth, and I moan my pleasure. The jeans are still around my ankles so I pull them away, turn around, and take them off. My ass is in your face and you take your fingers and push them under the string and into my slit, which is, of course, already dripping down my thighs. You push another finger in, and another and fuck me from behind. I lean on the table while you push and pull me close to orgasm. I hear you breathing—are you okay?"

"No. I want to come."

"While you fuck me, your pinky rubs against my clit and

you grab me with your other hand. You hold my ass tight and lean over me. I feel your tits bouncing around on my back, making your nipples hard. I hear you breathing in my ear."

"I'm going to come."

"No. I hear your breathing in my ear while you fuck me."

"I wanna come."

"No! Wait. I stand up and when you pull your hand out of me, I sit on the floor facing your bush, your clit, your dripping hole. You sit in front of me, too. We spread our legs apart and scoot closer to each other. I shove my fingers in you and reach for your incredible nipple with my free hand. You do the same and we become one, synchronized, hypnotized with each other's and our own pleasure. I feel you tighten baby. Do you feel me?"

"Yes!"

"I feel you get so tight and my own pussy tightens as a reflex to yours. We breathe in unison, we tighten in unison . . . Do you feel me?"

"Yes . . ."

"Are you ready?"

"Yes . . ."

"I let go of your nipple and lower my mouth to it—suck it in hard and you throw your head back . . ."

"Ohhhhh . . . Ohhhhh . . ."

"Oh my God . . ."

(breathes heavily)

"Oh my God . . ."

(breathing heavily)

"What baby?"

"I'm still huge."

"What?"

"My clit is still huge."

"Stay there, I'm on my way."

(Click!)

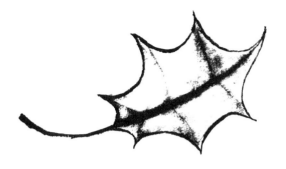

Autumn

Schoolgirls

Some stories are meant to be read aloud. This is one of those.

School days are filled with fantasies. Three women give in to theirs.

The teacher is late, but we know to keep writing in our journals instead of talking. But the tension between Anna and me is too much. Leslie, the other dyke in class, and I look at each other and know we could probably get away with it. My eyes beseech Anna's Asian ones and she gives me a slight nod, so we three get up and move to the empty desk in the corner. As Anna sits down, she lifts her skirt, revealing her nakedness. She is shaking, but I rub her legs as Leslie massages her neck. Leslie's hands unbutton Anna's blouse and feel her small breasts. Even though I'm between her legs, looking at, and occasionally feeling, her black, curly pubic hair, even though I'm between her legs and smelling her wonderful woman smells, the sight of Leslie on her breasts makes me jealous, so I reach up and touch her left breast. I shiver with pleasure. I adore breasts. Leslie has begun to kiss Anna's neck and I know we need to get on with it, if we are to finish before our teacher arrives. I see the other students writing diligently in their journals, so I return to Anna's puss.

My hands separate her thighs and follow her long legs downward to her boots. I kiss the place between vulva and thigh—that really tender spot—I lick, I suck. My tongue traces the right side of her pubic hair, over, across the top, and down the left side of her triangle. When I get to the bottom, my tongue tastes her dripping wetness. I lick, small gentle thrusts, parting her very wet lips. I see Leslie kissing Anna and push my tongue in further, kissing her myself. I touch the underside of her clit and feel her legs begin their uncontrollable quivering. I make the rotation to the top of her clit and put my lips on it and suck, drawing it in, letting it go, in and out. She likes this.

Oh these woman smells, woman tastes. My tongue finds her clit. After licking her fallen juices, I begin my slow spirals and am glad I'm down here and Leslie is up there. Her clit is hard and swollen and I feel her orgasm building. I'm fingering the entrance to her vagina and slide one finger in.

She moans, but Leslie covers Anna's mouth with her own. Another finger and Anna is about to explode. Her vagina is making those delightful pre-orgasm contractions. I use my fingers to feel and fill all of her. Around and around and around, I move my tongue to the right of her clit and circle there. Leslie's hands are on Anna's breasts, her fingers tightly around her nipples. Anna convulses as she orgasms, but we can restrain her and keep up our pleasures until she closes her legs on my head. I give her one last kiss and look at her. Leslie is already buttoning her blouse and I lick my lips. I let her dry on my hands. Anna, fairly composed, rises and pulls her skirt, her tight skirt, down. We are walking back to our desks as the teacher walks in and we begin our lessons for the day.

Tenuity

Hillary's making love to the thinner Leya brings about more than just another orgasm.

This short respite before I turn to make love to Leya is nice. I smell her sweat mixed with her shampoo. Such a lovely woman she is, so slight compared to my former lovers. In the past, my woman friends would be at least half as big as me—I thought a woman had to have substance to be able to stand up to me. When Leya came along, I realized my own prejudices about size.

Sweet Leya, a diminutive 120-pound woman who had a voice like an angel. I watched her perform at the Coffee House every Wednesday for two months before I felt courageous enough to say something to her. I'd sit reading a book, sipping tea, and (I felt, anyway) leering at her. Such a pretty aura that danced as she spoke of wrongs suffered, lessons learned, and unrequited love.

It was the unrequited love stuff I listened to most. I pictured crazy women haughtily walking away from her, or women oblivious to her glowing self as they stood next to her in the line. It wasn't until later, much later, that I learned she was the heartbreaker. I'm glad I didn't know the real truth because I probably would not have had the gumption to put my hand out to her as she walked by the table. But, I did, and after we talked for two hours that night, we made a date to see each other the next Saturday.

All day, we spoke of world peace, social issues, *kibbutzim*, vegetarianism, sexism, ageism, and an entire array of "politically correct" issues to discuss—including size-ism. Our views, in several areas, were extremely different, but a few we managed to agree on. What I liked, and we still relish, is how discussing the issues, no matter what our opinions are, is allowed and encouraged. Both of us like being separate people with some similar ideas.

After several months of dating (yes, dating! I know, an enigma in the lesbian community), we learned we had more in common than we had thought.

Leya and I love sex. I don't mean we just like it a whole lot, I mean we *love* it! Usually, one partner will have a higher libido than the other. Both Leya and I were the ones in our previous relationships who felt over-sexed at one time or another. This time though, we have found our equal.

I'm ready to pleasure Leya. I'm rested and so is she. I want to show her what it is I love in her.

I tell her I want to eat her first. She giggles and moves so I can rearrange myself. She lies down and is already clutching the sheets, even before I begin. I look up at her adoring face and am so glad I took the chance on a thinner woman. I was so afraid I'd crush her (in many aspects)—but she sure holds her own!

"Your eyes glitter like the stars, my lover."

"Oh, Hillary, you're just saying that so I'll love you more."

"Yup!"

"But, you see, I couldn't love you anymore than I do now, no matter what you say."

I feel all gooshy inside and decide we need a little more pre-lovin' since we had such a long rest. So, I slide off the bottom of the bed and take Leya's foot in my hands and stroke her toe hairs. Her toes are so small in my hand. I keep rubbing her foot and want to kiss it and am so glad we took a shower first. I lower my mouth to her big toe and kiss gently. Doing the same to each toe, I open my mouth and lick the outline of her foot, around the heel, and up the inside of her arch. She wriggles, but I know she is enjoying it.

I kiss/lick up her left leg and stretch my tongue to reach the underside of her knee. Such a tender spot, I love its softness. Once I'm at her inner thigh, I blow lightly on her wet mound. I see that making love to me has excited her a little (a lot!) and it turns me on. Leya tells me the air is cold when I blow, so I use my tongue and make one long lick up her puss. She arches, grasps the sheets hard, and lets out a loud moan. I laugh and smile up at her. I turn my attention to her right leg; kiss/lick down her thigh, under her knee, around her arch, her heel, her outer foot. Then, I kiss each toe, the little one first, and end on her big toe. I stroke my good-byes on her toe hairs and move back up on the bed between her thighs.

I inhale deeply and can almost taste her muskiness. She's so wet, the aroma is thick in the air. My fingers separate her lips and I see the folds opening for me. My finger dips in, and when I push, it disappears.

"Where does it go?" I ask out loud.

"To my soul," she answers.

So I move in and out to touch her soul more often. When I pull my finger out, I see her clitoris, her "pink lady." I am hungry for her, so I swoop down and devour the swollen nodule. I feel the sheet leave the mattress and push my hand in once again. Leya, who has been excited since we were at the store, has her third , but not last, orgasm of the evening. I feel her pulsing, and on an open pulse, I push two fingers in her. Only when she's this excited can she take two fingers because they are so fat. Lying here, fucking her, she doesn't mind—and actually loves—my fatness.

I do not remove my fingers but get up and maneuver onto my left hand and knees so Leya can enter me. My breasts dwarf hers and I feel the pressure I put on her body. (I've teased her by saying my nipples are bigger than her whole breast.) She loves me on her—I get great leverage so I can fuck her hard while she fucks me.

Oh, in and out with each other.

Are we separate? Is that me about to come, or her? I feel her cervix as she feels mine.

Tight, tight, tight.

Yes, we both orgasm at the same time. My grunting is synchronized with her groaning. I want to come again; I love this feeling, but I want her to hang over me.

We shift positions, and as she dangles a breast over my mouth, I grab it with my lips. I reach between her thighs and insert a finger, not two fingers because her puss tightens up as soon as I leave it. I play with her nipple as if it were her clitoris and love the feel of it between my teeth. Apparently, she loves it, too. She's making lovely sounds, guttural and sexy. We fuck each other good, and within seconds, come again.

Oh, she is so incredible! Her body on mine . . .

"I want to party. Want to party with me?"

"Of course!" as she reaches over my head for the vibrator. Her other breast falls into my mouth and I suck it in. She says, "Wait!" and pulls our toy out of its hiding place in the headboard.

She hands it to me and I turn it on. I'm the conductor, so she waits until I've situated myself before lowering her pelvis onto mine.

How wonderful we thought we were discovering two-on-a-vibrator. Giddy with laughter afterwards, we couldn't believe it hadn't dawned on us earlier. We have since seen ads for two-headed vibrators and have considered buying one, but we always look at the one we have and say, "Naw . . ." So we're sentimental too. Oh, well . . .

I get the attachment on my clit and Leya rests her puss (and her clit, too, I imagine) on the back of the vibrator. I push that button to high and *love* the jiggles it gives me. Leya needs it on the lower speed, so the subtle twitching the vibrator's back affords is perfect for her.

Leya lies on me. We rock together, sometimes whispering I love you's, sometimes moaning or verbalizing loudly, and sometimes silent, deep within ourselves, or deep within each other.

I can feel her clit on my hand (it's really on the toy) and it excites me. Oh, does it excite me! I love Leya's movements, her fluid back and forth on the vibrator. She tells me she feels me, too. Engorgement is incredible in my puss, and hers. I feel the orgasm spreading through my ass and thighs. I feel so high with this woman I love. I want to come with her again, so I tell her. Weeeeee—she is right there with me!

Off we go into our souls and converging with each other's. Vibrator orgasms last as long as we lie merged together; and I can make Leya come again simply by coaxing her.

"You feel wonderful." And I reach under her with my left hand to tug on her nipple—and yes, she comes again.

Once Leya lifts off of me, I turn the switch off and move the vibrator to the bed. She lays back down on me and we kiss and nuzzle before falling asleep.

Such ferocity and intensity in my Leya. I will never regret my decision to learn about who she is and what she stands for. In discovering her secrets, I have also learned the world is not the only place prejudice exists. I saw it in myself.

Here's to eliminating stereotypes!

My own included.

Beyond Words

Tess, a hearing woman, and her long-time lover, Maggie, a deaf woman, learn that pleasures continue to grow in a committed relationship and that love transcends different capabilities.

Pulling Tess toward the dance floor was a feat in itself. Hundreds of women blocked the way, either engaged in conversation or themselves frantically flailing about. I saw a spot ahead and knew I had to move fast or I would lose it to a gyrating woman threatening to expand her spacial parameters. I felt the thump, thump, thump of the bass and the more subtle vibrations of the various shades of music and all of them together made me want to dance. Closing my eyes, I could become one with the music and my body enjoyed the stimulation. I am careful to keep both feet on the floor so I get the full effect, almost like a body vibrator, but I also love to partner-dance: two step, disco, and ballroom. Feeling the music is one thing I can do as a deaf woman that doesn't make me stand out. Although I love seeing what words go with the music, the beat is what turns me on.

Tess runs her hands up and down on my body, exciting me, teasing me. She tells me she will have her way with me later and tosses her head back to laugh. I enjoy her pleasure and tell her I will enjoy every moment of it. I close my eyes again and am absorbed in the pulsation and imagine Tess touching my body, later when we are both free of our clothes. I feel her rub my ass and picture her between my thighs while holding my ass tight in her hands. I see her tongue reach out for me and feel it make contact with my clitoris. Such an incredible feeling! I'm aroused beyond belief. Tess taps me on the shoulder and I, reluctantly, open my eyes. "Maggie, where are you?" she signs. I show her where I was and her eyes open wide with surprise. "Is that what you have in your mind?" I nod. "Do you want to go home?" "Not yet. I still want to dance. Such big beats feel good. You know we can't do this at home because the neighbors have a fit." "Okay. I want you, too, so as soon as you're ready, let me know and we'll go."

After another hour of dancing, I'm ready to go home with the woman I love. On the way home, she cuddles up to me and traces the outline of my breast with her finger. I feel my nipple harden and it's hard to keep my eyes on the road. Pushing her hand gently away, I tell her to wait. I'm a little tired now and need to concentrate on getting us home. When we get there, we go different ways, knowing we'll be close again very soon. I check the TDD for messages and Tess checks the answering machine. We've been together so long, it's great to have a routine worked out and our strengths and weaknesses recognized. I'm much better with money than she is. She loves the frivolous; anything we have to dust before company comes, little goodies for friends, pretty odds and ends we have absolutely no use for. Tess is definitely better with the aesthetic. All those knick knacks she acquired before I came around decorate our home beautifully. Her sense of style rivals what I've seen in magazines. I love it when she shops for me because I know I will always be the recipient of exquisite gifts at Solstice and on birthdays. Both of us enjoy people and our home is quite the haven for friends needing a safe space or for women in the throes of a break-up. So few people know ASL. Tess encourages everyone to learn, but until they do, she is my, and their, interpreter.

Tonight, though, we are alone, the cats are fed, and we go upstairs to play. I watch Tess as she takes her hair out of the rubber band. The gray streaks are barely perceptible unless I'm holding her in my arms. I tell her how lovely she is and I watch her sign "Thank you" and lower her eyes demurely. She flips her head down and brushes the tangles out of her hair as I gaze intently, waiting for her to flip her head back up. Her hair is wild when she does that and it excites me. As soon as she does it, I move to prevent her from brushing it any more. I take the brush out of her hand and lay it on the counter. She tells me she wasn't done with that and I explain to her how enticing she is with her hair out of place. She turns to look at herself in the mirror and strikes a model's pose. "Yes, I guess I do look disheveled," she signs, but fingerspells "disheveled" to make sure I understand that she isn't just messy. I sign to her reflection in the mirror, "I don't really care how you look, I love you," and I put my arms around her waist and my hands hold her breasts. Immediately, her nipples become erect and I take each nipple between my thumbs and forefingers and feel their hardness. I want to feel them in my mouth, so I turn her around and lower my mouth to her left breast. She has freckles and moles and little black hairs that give her breasts more character than my own. She told me she spent years plucking her hairs and then stopped when I encouraged her to. I'm glad she did. I lick around her areola and relish the different sensations her breast offers me. I radiate in smaller and smaller circles and eventually find myself at the center, her pebble-hard nipple. I suck in as much of her breast as I can and play using my tongue. I feel her inhale deeply and know she must be making noises I can't hear. I place my hand on her throat and, as she moans, I feel the vibrations that excite me even more. I lift my head and ask Tess if we could move to the bed. She says, "Yes!" and we hold hands while we walk there.

I feel the water underneath me and enjoy the floating sensation. I remember the first time I laid in a waterbed, I couldn't believe a bed could move so much. It feels so slow and sensual, a feeling I enjoy immensely. Tess and I lie naked together and I admire her soft body. She has muscles underneath her ample flesh so I feel the power under her softness. She asks me what I'm thinking and I roll over onto my belly and take her nipple in my mouth once again. My hand slides down her belly and I let my forefinger wriggle in her belly button for a moment. Her stomach convulses and I look up to see her laughing. I lift up and ask her if she likes that and she tells me she enjoys tickling for only a moment or two. I had done it just long enough. I smile at her and sign that I love learning all these little things, that I had thought I knew it all. She tells me I will never know it all. I say, "Good." I lower myself onto her other breast and resume the descent with my right hand. Her pubic area is highlighted with a delightful bunch of hairs, some straight and some curly. They don't seem to follow any pattern and every time I put my hand there, it is like I am feeling it for the first time. I keep my fingers busy trying to find her clitoris, which is well-hidden. After I spread her lips apart, I have easier access to her wet and her clitoris. Once I touch her wet, I sit up and tell her I can't wait any longer. I tell her how beautiful she was dancing and that image I had of her eating me is haunting me. She tells me she is eager to eat me also and suggests we do our "body kiss," what others call 69. A shiver runs through my body and I fingerspell a slow, sensuous Y-E-S, I W-A-N-T Y-O-U.

Tess pulls me to her and she kisses me deeply, filled with heat. I like Tess on top so all the gravity can pull her body down on me and I can feel every muscle and detect every intake of breath. When I explained that to her (she was used to being on the bottom because she is usually heavier than her lovers), she told me she would do it, but if she was mooshing me, I just needed to tap her three times and she would move. We have done our "body kiss" that way every time and I have never had a problem. In fact, once Tess understood enough sign language and I could explain all the different sensations I am aware of while she is lying on top of me and when she comes, she told me she was jealous that she wasn't as sensitive as I am. I told her tough luck!

So, when I pull back from our kiss, Tess gets up and I lie down with my head flat on the bed. Tess turns around and I watch her lift her leg over my shoulders and plant a knee on either side of my body. I can see the grand sight of her entire behind and vulva in my face and my clit swells immediately. Not only do I see her clit, her lips, her mound of pubic hair, but also her ass and the tiny hole, we never touch or seem to talk about but I enjoy watching, that contracts and relaxes according to her level of pleasure while I eat her. My attention is diverted by Tess's face in my crotch and I feel her hot mouth ready itself to lower onto my most private area. When I close my eyes, I can become engulfed in the sensations. We rock up and down with the rhythm of the bed and with each other trying to get our tongues in deeper. This feeling of body kissing is so wonderful. I feel like I'm floating on a cloud in the air, and I'm so incredibly turned on, I can hardly stand the waiting. I force myself to concentrate on Tess and her pleasure so I can prolong my own. I feel her dripping into my mouth and I suck her openness so I may, momentarily, consume her. I push my tongue in as deeply as it will reach and I feel the underside of it strain. I know that tomorrow I will have a good case of Lezzie Tongue, but I don't care. I push in deeper. As I do, I feel Tess's vibrations starting near my vulva and radiating out toward my chest. I know she must be making growling noises because they always start in her throat and, as she gets more excited, they come from her entire chest and belly. My tongue moves out of the wet it craves so it can feel my lover's clit. I want to know what it does to her to stick my tongue in so deep. I am surprised by the enormity of her clit and promptly begin to ravish it. Tess rises up slightly and I know to ease up on her too-sensitive nub. I have to curb my passion for a moment. Get control. Then, slowly reach out, touch lightly, and make her want it harder. I flick my tongue on what I picture are the ends of the nerve center of her body. I can just see all the nerve trails leading to the source, and I, the greatest explorer of all time, have kept my secret all to myself. This is my salvation, my heaven, my fountain of youth, and no one except the Goddess herself can share in the external pleasures I have rediscovered.

My rich fantasy must be affecting Tess because she is writhing about on top of me. Her clit is a hard, pulsating Being in my mouth and I know she is going to soon come for me. I want to come with her tonight. Most times I let her come alone because I love focusing all my love, my concentration of power. Tonight, though, I keep thinking about the two of us on the dance floor and how smoothly we move together, how fluid our motions and our bodies are. I take Tess's pleasure as my own and I feel her mouth on my clit. Something that had been a vague sensation is now a dramatic pressure aching to find release.

We have become. In these few moments before we lose ourselves to the universe, we become one with it. As we talk about universal energy and the oneness of everyone, Tess and I become the embodiment of whole consciousness. We get so high and beg to linger for just a moment longer. Before we slip into earthly unconsciousness, we are over. We flow between this world and the next and it feels like it must feel to the hawk as she soars above the earth; all sensations and yet, none can be explained. Lower and lower we glide until she puts us back in our place on our waterbed in our home and in our own bodies.

Tess turns around and kisses me while tears drip on my face and neck. I squeeze my eyes to let my own tears drop to the bed and ask her if she felt what I felt. She can only nod and heaves a sigh that leaves me to wonder if she really did. My darling lays her head on my chest and I know, because she has told me so many times, that she is listening to my heart beating. I feel drops falling and rivulets sliding down to my back. I can only hold her until she is ready to, or able to, talk.

We have napped and Tess pulls herself up from my body. Her tear-stained face moves me and I tell her I love her with all my heart by signing "I Love You" and laying my hand on the place she has just left. She signs that she loves me also, with all her heart, and keeps signing that she has never felt so much at one time in all her life, not even when we were first lovers and we didn't leave bed for two weeks. I remember that and tell her I know what she means, that was wonderful, but this was spiritual. I see recognition in her eyes and she says, "Yes! That was it!" I ask her if she would like to shower with me and continue our conversation amid the falls. She says she would, so our words are continued as if in a driving rain, mingling with the water and the emotion, yet easily understood by both of us. We have both felt that today was a day of startling realities and precious memories. Neither of us is quite sure of how the profound message the spirits hold for us will manifest itself, but we both agree we are open and waiting and filled with anticipation for any gift the Mother has to give.

Winter

Morning Glory

Cold mornings sometimes provide the best settings for hot beginnings.

I love waking up with you. Your face in sleep is relaxed and beautiful. I feel grateful when you open your eyes and smile. "At me! She smiles at me!" Desire shoots to and through my body. I reach out to touch you and your hand is already open, waiting to receive mine. I scoot over to you and our warmth under the heavy covers is reassuring.

Curling into you, I smell you—the mixtures of us from last night, dampness from the heat, and you—your smell. I feel comforted, at home, and the desire to have you again continues to rise. My right hand has your hand and my left finds your breast, your nipple. You say, "Hi" in your husky, morning voice and I lower my mouth to your breast to drink my good morning from you. Your moan encourages me and I look up with your nipple still in my mouth and smile. I let go for a moment to tell you, "I want you." You reply, "You've got me." And I say to myself, "And so I do." My hand slides from yours down to your belly and my fingers find your short hairs between your legs. As if by reflex, your legs move apart and I continue playing, scratching softly, separating your folds. I continue my nuzzling of your breast—licking softly, then harder, encouraging hardness in several places on your body. I want your tongue so I move up and look in your eyes. How exquisitely beautiful you are! I drink from your eyes and my lips touch yours. My eyes close and I feel the soft, wet heat of your tongue on mine. I can always imagine the feeling of your tongue on my clit when we kiss. Our tongues move, swirls of love, swirls of warmth, swirls of pleasure, circle you, circle me, circle our very being. I feel my body swell and open and I ready myself for you. I feel the sweat on the back of my neck and the backs of my knees. My fingers dipping into your slit are getting wet and you press still closer to me.

Your hands have been exploring my terrain and now they have found my breasts . . . your fingers have found my nipples—and they twirl! Your fingers pull and tug, while I feel amazing surges of energy in my groin. My mind lets go of you and I concentrate on the feelings in me. Your fingers are animals devouring my inhibitions and I feel the beginnings of an orgasm. I'm surprised because my breasts aren't usually so sensitive, but I consciously let go of the thought and just feel. Hearing your breathing overlaid with mine excites me even more. Because you are getting pleasure out of mine, I am high beyond belief and wet gushes freely from my puss.

O beautiful woman. You who can make me come just with the exchange of energy from hands to breast! How can I tell you how you make me feel? As I release, I pull you to my body, bury my face in your neck, smell your hair, and I feel your vein pulsate as you, too, relax from my orgasm.

I want to cry sometimes, you make me so happy. The emotion is so great!

I want you to come, too, so I again touch the wet of your essence. My fingers swirl around your clitoris—my mouth aches to touch it—so I suck your nipple into my mouth and let it simulate, and stimulate, your clit. I love it when you pull me close like that. My tongue flicks and plays with your nipple, making it swell in unison with your clit. Holding me close, your breath begins to heave and I know you are nearing orgasm. Your clitoris swells to triple its resting size and I am frantic in my touching and licking. Arching, you shudder in my arms and I let out the breath I have been holding, waiting for you to come. Both of us, sweating from all the work so early in the morning, huddle together in silence before reality reminds us of our responsibilities. The children's low giggles tell us our day has begun. One last kiss, the squeeze of a hand, and off we go!

The Letter

Kiah's pain provokes an insightful letter reminding Jerica of the memories, and the sex, she walked away from. Before Kiah seals the envelope, she discovers strengths she did not know she possessed.

17 September, 1990

Jerica,

How much I miss you. As I write this, I know you are missing me, too. We had so much fun in our four years together.

Do you remember when we first fell in love?

You told me how beautiful my eyes were, that you got lost in the shadows of my iris. I remember how much fun we had in bed, snuggled in the cornflower blue sheets, your cocoa-colored skin shining, asking for more of me. I gave to you willingly. I still do. How can you ignore what we have shared? Why won't you answer my calls? I decided to write to you since my messages on your machine even go unheeded.

I always loved holding your hand. You are so strong, so powerful. Taking your fingers in my mouth, I would curl my tongue around them and suck. How I pulled nourishment from them, I'll never know, but I did. I would feel your knuckles, lick your nails, kiss the "V"s in between your fingers. Once I filled myself of their goodness, I moved up to your wrist. Remember that first time my tongue touched it? You told me no one had ever done that to you. You can't say that anymore, can you?

I can taste you, Jer, I can taste your salt and your sweet. I can see your shoulder and feel my hand caressing you. I see your braids and am glad your hair is up so I have easy access to your delicious neck. Licking the raw nerves of your throat begins your moaning. I loved how noisy you got. Come be noisy for me again, baby. My hands slide under your shirt and touch the underside of your breast. It is so soft, softer than almost any part of your body.

Almost.

I lift your shirt and lower my head to your nipple. I look at it before opening my mouth. Your deep brown nipple is already swelling, simply from my gaze. I move closer, stretch my mouth wide, and lean forward, embracing your breast with my tongue. Your softness and hardness blend together and I press my nose into your flesh so I can inhale you and your scent. Flicks of my tongue affect your breathing—I feel a shudder of pleasure run through your body. I lift your shirt over your other breast, the one you say is smaller. My hand distinguishes no difference and plays enticing games similar to the ones my mouth is enjoying. You start to lean sideways on the couch and I know we won't stop for hours. (Do you remember, my sensuous Jerica, when we made love in the hot tub in Colorado, and when you leaned sideways, you submerged yourself? We laughed so hard! The snow around the tub kept us in the water until we were both wrinkled raisins, remember?)

Before you lie down, I lift your shirt over your head, and as my right hand lays it on the floor, my left one reaches out for the button on your jeans. I work it free and, slowly, unzip you from your confining clothes. You lie back, head on the arm of the couch, and watch while I pull your pants down, over your butt, over your knees, and off—socks on or off? "Off," you say. Off it is.

You are lying on our couch, one leg raised, the other extended. Your beauty moves me. I start to kiss your shin and you pat the couch beside you. I won't fit, so I kneel on the floor and start to kiss your underbreast. You stop me once again and tell me you want me naked, too. Shedding my clothes, I feel how cool the house is, but I don't care. I know we'll both be sweating within the hour.

I resume my kneeling position and now you let me kiss your breast. My right hand strokes the tendrils at your temples while my left hand strokes the tendrils of your mound. You are so beautiful as I peek at you—so incredibly erotic.

My fingers start spreading your lips apart and I hear the sticky wet that waits for me. I need you. I need your puss in my face. Lifting off of your nipple, I motion for you to sit up and scootch down so I can sit and feast from my position on the floor. You comply and I relish in your woman scent of musk today. I bow to brush my cheek against your thigh. You shiver and I turn my face, reaching out with my tongue and to lick from upper thigh to where your thigh and pelvis join. I circle this place, visualizing your clitoris, until I can no longer stand the waiting.

I push your thighs apart and lean into your space and kiss. Starting with chaste kisses and slowly becoming more sensual, more wet, I kiss your whole vulva. Periodically, my tongue touches the deep velvet recesses of your vagina. The tartness of your insides prompts me to suck, lick, probe still deeper. I feel your clit on the bridge of my nose. I know the pressure is causing it to grow and, reluctantly, I pull my tongue out to experience your "blueberry." (Do you remember when we named it? I couldn't think of what it felt like; hard, yet smooth, round, juicy, and a lovely shade of reddish-blue with a brown hood. You said I described a blueberry in a basket. I asked "If I ate it, would it disappear?" You said no, that it would always be there. I wish it were here now.)

How I wish I could taste, lick, eat, smell, and suck every part of you at once. This is the one time I wish we weren't monogamous so I , and the others, could pleasure you all over, all at the same time. I would station one woman on your mouth—feed you tongue or puss as your desire leads. Another would be sucking your breast—could there be two, one for each breast? I, of course, would claim your pulsing vagina, but I can still see one more woman sucking on your toes. You and I know how you love that! I love bringing you pleasure. You have to know that.

But, I am alone with you. No other woman is here to help me make love to you.

I am really all alone and wishing I was with you. Reading this, don't you recall our love? Can it be so easy for you to walk away? Why aren't you here? Were our differences so great? I hear you screaming at me to get a life—to leave you alone. You are my life, don't you understand? I haven't known what to do with myself since you've gone. I've read books that are supposed to help—and all I do is cry.

Why am I telling you this? You always hated my tears.

I was so proud when you started AA. I thought our lives would be happy—happier. I didn't know you would change so much. Sometimes I wish you'd never gone. Isn't that selfish? I feel so mean when I think that. I should be thrilled at your sobriety and yet, I find myself fantasizing about bringing you elegant bottles of Southern Comfort served up in brandy snifters. Somehow I think you'll love me drunk. You loved me before.

I feel your "blueberry," your clitoris, in my mouth. I look at it and see how swollen it is. My tongue flicks lightly on it and you squirm. You tell me to eat you and I take your nub in my mouth, between my lips, and suck. My tongue slides over and over, around and around. I feel your hand on my head, pressing me into you—begging me to suck harder. I move my right hand and feel with my fingers how wet you are. I want to be in you, so I slide two fingers in and begin my frigging. We liked that word better than fucking; it was more lesbian-friendly. My hand and my mouth are synchronized and my left hand reaches up to fondle your heaving breast. You arch, but still cling to my head and I send you loving energy.

Do you feel it? I send it to you when I masturbate. I alternate eating you or having you make love to me.

I know you are going to come—your thighs close around my head and I hear no sound. I hear the blood pulsing in my brain and feel you—so tight. Your clit swells and I feel you shake uncontrollably as you come and spill your wet into my waiting palm. I let go of your clit and dive into the waves. My mouth splashes, using my tongue to lap up your delightful juices.

You pull me up to you and I float into your arms. We kiss, darting tongues and nipping lips, and I tell you how much I want to come.

(You used to love making love to me. You taught me how to use a vibrator. I never had before you. That was the first purchase after you left, my own toy. I loved it when you made me come with it.)

You go to our room and get Desiree and bring it back to the couch. Plugged in, she begins to hum. I lie back and you use your left hand to spread my lips, exposing my clitoris. Desiree finds her way to the left of my clit and *zap!*, she's on me, pushing me, urging me along to my orgasm. Jerica, I feel your breath on my thigh and vulva. I feel the energy you possess as you guide Desiree to my wanting puss. I feel the intense warmth creeping up my ass and spreading over my thighs and I feel my clit, suddenly, against the vibrator's head. I am gone—a frenzy of sensations flow through my body. I hear your "Yes, baby. Yes, baby," and come some more.

I'm crying again. Ever since you left, I've fantasized about you, and only you. Last night I felt the feelings of pleasure, but I couldn't find you. Where were you? I'll bet you're glad.

We had so many wonderful memories. Yes, I know, a few awful ones, too. But, I know we could make things better again.

Come here, love. Touch my hand. Feel my love. I have so much love—I always expected to share it with you. Answer my calls. Please answer this letter.

I love you.

Kiah

P.S. 22 September, 1990

Jerica,

I've sat on this letter for five days and have tried sealing it every day. I read and re-read it and now I've read it so much, what is the meaning?

I do love you Jerica, but the more I write, cry, spend time alone—the more I heal. Healing for me means thinking less and less about you and more and more about me. Do you understand? I think you do. I hear "Finally!" travelling across the city and, I have to tell you, I agree. I am a wonderful woman. Reading how I loved you and realizing I will be able to love another, soothes me greatly. I have so much to do: my groups, my writing, my photography. These are things I set aside when we got together. Was that wrong to focus on you, on *us* so much? Maybe we just didn't know any better. I can't believe how different I feel today compared to last week when I wrote the letter. I thought about tearing it up, but vetoed that idea. It's just as good for you, as it is for me, to see that I can process, too!

Will I falter and cling and grope for answers? I'm sure I will. But, what I said in the first part of the letter, the one glaring phrase to me was—"You are my life, don't you understand?"

Well, Jerica, I have a vague, obscure feeling, more like a seed of a feeling, that says, "Kiah, *you* are important to you."

I hear it, and now I think I understand. No one else is my life.

I am my life.

Thank you for the lesson. Good luck. I will always love you.

Your friend,

Kiah

Regeneration

I hung on to Grandma Ceil's words like a child hangs on to a tire swing. I'd watched her and Grandma Fanny work 'round the house, fixin' the chair, repairin' the washer—both workin' after they's done workin' they's real jobs down to the plant. Grandma Ceil done'd the screwy part of the thing-a-ma-jig they built, and Grandma Fanny kept the toilets cleaned. I knowed they was dif'rent 'cuz'n I heard "Lezzie!" shouted at each of 'em at separate times. I didn't care 'cuz I turned out to be a lezzie, too.

They both musta' knowed I was a little lezzie child 'cuz they doted on me and loved me even when I was a rascally gal. They'd laugh and elbow each other and say, "Looks like we got us one!" I like bein' able to make 'em laugh, they's life was so hard and all.

When I growed up enough, I used to ask 'em stories 'bout how they falled in love. They'd look at each other, and I swear, they's eyes would get all soft and wet. I used to wanna cry when they doed that. They's loved each other, I could tell. But my constant askin' didn't get no quick or easy answer outta them. I'd have to pry and make myself nosy to get any answer outta them swoonin' women.

"Well," Grandma Ceil would start, "we's little girls who lived down the ways from each other and we'd meet down the crik to gets us some water. I's lovin' her since'n I was 7, 8 years old. It took her amight piece longer. How old was you anyway, when you finally said you'd be my girl?"

Grandma Fanny took her sweetheart's fragile hand and said, "Why, I always been yours."

I knowed she was a lyin' 'cuz she'd got married an' had my mama an' been a widow 10 years 'fore she moved in with Grandma Ceil, mama'd tole me. She said she's 11 when the scandal hit and kids was throwin' oranges at 'er to make 'er feel rotten for havin' lezzie mamas. She'd said they'd tried to be hidden 'bout it, but bein' in a small town like Opelika, everyone knowed what they was doin' even 'fore they did!

My grandmas is hearty women—they don't take no crap (pardon my fierceness) off'n nobody. They marched to each house and personally told everyone it 'twas none a nobody's business who lived with who as long as the house was clean and the yard was kept. If two lonely women and a child couldn't live together in peace, who could? Mama says 'cuz they showed gumption, the town piped down. Kids didn't throw no oranges no more and life went on as before, but now she had two mamas 'stead a daddy and a mama.

I think 'bout all I gotta face bein' a lezzie way out here in the wet heat near the palmetto bushes and the cock-aroaches. Where do I find me a lady friend? Do I's go to the crik for water, too? Is that where I find me someone to love? It's amazin' to me that they's ever find each other way out here next to nowhere.

I keep askin' questions 'cuz my grandmas is gettin' old. I'm nearin' thirty-one and my mama's fifty-two. Grandma Ceil's sixty-nine and Grandma Fanny's seventy-three. I's still alone an' I wanna find out how they knowed one another. I also wanna know what private things they shared. A feelin' comes over me and I jus' gotta know somethin', 'cuz if I don't, I might never find out. I wonder where that feelin' creeps up from.

I jest might be gettin' farther with gettin' answers. I go to the depot in Montgomery to work for a couple a' weeks at a time an' when I come back, my grandmas is softer. They's skin is softer, they's hair is softer, even they's eyes is softer. I's led to believe old folks got hard—not these here old folks. They be pillows 'fore too long.

One time, upon my return, my grandmas sits me down and starts talkin'—without my even askin'! I's so surprised, I sat dumbfounded while they each took turns tellin' me a story. After while, I thought I should have some paper and a pencil or somethin' so's I could keep a note of what they said. They talked so many stories it was hard to keep each one in a kind a' order. When I moved to shift my butt around the chair they snapped at me to sit still. Said I was actin' like when I was two—and off they'd go, on another story. Once, when I had to pee, I had to raise my hand like a school girl. I took my time in the outhouse so I could breathe my own air for a minute. I walked slow-like back to the house and prepared for more. Already I'd heard stories of odd jobs: paintin' here for Clem down the road, bakin' for Miz Nell 'cuz she's always down with child, haulin' folks to town or outta town for varyin' reasons. I'd heard tell about when I was no bigger'n a grasshopper's knee and throw'd up my breakfast on the Reverend's wife on Easter Sunday. I'd heard tell 'bout my first fall outta tree. Grandma Ceil came an' fetched me off the roots where I'd hit my head and carry'd me in an' nursed me good 'till I was kickin' an' screamin' to climb that same tree again. I'd heard 'bout uppity white folks and their meanness and hate for the Africans. My grandmas bein' so dif'rent themselves, fought for everyone who needed fightin' for. They'd soon fetch a cat outta the well 'fore they'd fetch the granny for the uppity Miz Porter down by the river. I learnt 'bout the dif'rent peoples who lived 'round here: the Indians who was here 'fore white folks, the Spaniards who came an' took the land, the Africans who was dragged here 'gainst they's will, and the dif'rent white folks. We was poor.

We is poor, so we is considered white trash. Grandmas tole 'bout makin' me Sunday dresses outta 'tater sacks an' how I'd prance 'round like a silly girl. Them rich folks who sat in the pretty pews, while we stood in the back, looked their nose up at us. Specially after Grandma Fanny decided she'd had enough of they's snobbery and sat in that front pew next to the Reverend's wife where I solidly spilled my stomach on her yellow silk dress. She was a sight, they say, a god-fearin' woman strugglin' with her mad—it jest achin' to get out! My grandmas was laughin' so hard in the tellin', I's thought they's gonna faint. Once'd they'd got control of theyselves, they looked plumb sober. I's still wipin' tears from my eyes from the laughin' and the way they look done scared me. I ast what were wrong and they took each other's hand and I watched those laugh tears turn to cry tears. I was 'fraid. Grandma Fanny, the one who stomped 'round the most 'bout my mama being hit with the oranges—the one who ain't 'fraid of nuthin'—Grandma Fanny said, kinda matter-a-factly, "I's dyin'." I watched her push that stubborn tear off her cheek but I couldn't see no more 'cuz my own tears was in the way. I ast, "How you know? Who'd say a damn fool thing like that anyways?"

Grandma Ceil said it were true. She said she'd gone to the granny who felt a big apple in her woman parts and sent her to that uppity doctor in Birmingham. It'd took two weeks a travelin' to learn the fact that nothin' could be done an' she's dyin'.

Both my grandmas was strokin' my hair 'cuz I falled on my knees at their feet, sobbin' like a baby jest born. They tole me to get 'holda myself so they could tell me they's private business they'd never tole me. Talkin' amongst theyselves while I blew my nose on a big white hankie, they aloud wondered why they didn't answer my questions the hundret times I ast b'fore. "'Cuz we's private folk, even if we do have us one in our midst."

I don't know if it were the moment or what, but I broke out with lamentin' 'bout not havin' no one like they did, how I looked everywhere and could never find no woman to love like they'd love each other. They said to jest wait. My time'd come, patience bein' a virtue an' all.

They'd commence on tellin' me 'bout they's private business and, now that I's hearin' it, I's embarrassed. What made me think I wanted to hear all this? They's tellin' me 'bout their money situation and how they'd made a will with a lawyer in Birmingham, how they'd had just a little bit set aside and I'd get it once they's both passed on. I said I didn't want no money, I jest wanted them. They chuckled wasn't I sweet.

Then they tole me 'bout they's lovin'. I'd thought I's embarrassed b'fore when they talk surrounded money—'twas nothin' compared to listenin' to their lovin'. They's tellin' me 'bout they's 'tractions and how sweet like candy each thought they was when they's behind closed doors. I fought from bein' terribly embarrassed an' listened like they wasn't my grandmas so I could see 'bout learnin' they's secret.

I heard tell 'bout strawberries appearin' on each other's front porches, 'bout the yard bein' swept and eggs done plucked from the hens waitin' to be cracked. They talked 'bout lazy days with my mama down the crik—they's ol' water heaven where'd they first see each other and liked each other's hair braids. They's kissin' when they's ten an' fourteen years old, but Fanny got scared when she heared the Reverend's sermon 'bout it bein' a sin an' all doin' stuff that ain't in the holy wedlock and 'twasn't 'till ten years after my grandpa died that she and Ceil had theyselves they own ceremony—jest 'tween God and theyselves. Then they knowed they's kissin' wadn't no sin no more. 'Course, folks wanderin' in or outta town would talk down they's vows, but the folks that knowed 'em would jest not listen and said, "You don't know for what you speak, so jest you shut up," and they's did.

Grandma Ceil tol' me how, 'fore they had they's wedlock ceremony, how she always jest waited for Fanny to come 'round. She said she watched her close like—'specially when she's with child, takin' her food to make sure she get plenty. Nosy folks ast if she's wantin' to granny that baby, sayin' she's a better one, pay more 'tention than the real granny who birthed babies. Ceil try to stay away when folks talk like that, but felt pulled to her like a bee to flower. When Ceil bringin' her collards one day, spiced heavy with bacon, Fanny were big with the baby. They's not able to stay 'way from each other and Fanny tol' Ceil she were scared 'bout this baby-havin'. Grandpa was out plowin' the field so Ceil felt careful 'bout comin' 'round so close and slyly touches Fanny's hand for a comfort. Fanny turned 'round sideways and Ceil come close to her face. Grandma Ceil an' Grandma Fanny both start talkin' at the same time as if neither heared t'other. Talkin' 'bout they smell so sweet, how's they could hear they breathin' goin' in an' out. They both would like'd to faint it was so powerful. As Fanny leaned to kiss Ceil, she was awfully embarrassed 'cause her water bag done broke all over Ceil's feet and Fanny's floor. The sweetness was gone for Fanny buckled over and hollered 'bout her mama havin' babies quick an' all. Ceil set Fanny down the chair an' ran to fetch Grandpa to fetch the granny. Ceil ran back an' stayed helpin' Fanny, puttin' rags on her head an' coverin' her with quilts, an' frettin' 'bout where'n tarnation that granny is. Grandma Fanny commenced to tellin' me 'bout how Ceil were a good granny and when mama's head were comin' out her woman part, Ceil jest reached down there an' kept that girl baby from fallin' on the floor. Mama laid on Grandma Fanny's tit and et her first feedin' 'fore the granny showed up to finish the birthin' of the afterbirth. You'd a thought Grandma Ceil done had mama, the way she looked tellin' and hearin' the story. She so proud!

After the initial joy waned a bit, Fanny was a-scared of what sign her water bag breakin' was when she leaned to sin again. Took a whole heap a' convincin' 'fore she said "she do" to Ceil's proposin'—10 years a' convincin'!

My two grandmas sat there a tellin' me 'bout they's honeymoonin' time. I was powerful shy 'bout hearin' it, but sat still.

Grandma Fanny talked 'bout Ceil's hen-colored hair and how the sun set in it every night. I could jus' 'bout see my Grandma Ceil flush up a bit. Grandma Fanny continued, talkin' 'bout the way Ceil walk, the way she push her hair outta her face when sweat keep pullin' it down. I heard tell 'bout Ceil's lovin' food. Fanny ain't never tasted nothin's good as Ceil's fried chicken, sweet 'taters, and them collards with bacon spices. Ceil jump in with, "Aw, that's all I knows how to fix. You's the one who bakes all them good treats: pineapple upside-down cake, peach cobbler, an' my very fav'rite—pecan pie!" Fanny says we gettin' off the track she wanted to wander down. She want to talk 'bout lovin' each other, 'bout how many dif'rent ways they is to show lovin'. She says lovin' jest 'taint in the dark with the door closed. She wanted to tell Ceil how the ways she love her in front a' me 'cuz when she gone, Ceil might forget. Ceil lettin' her tears fall and sayin' she ain't never gonna forget. She had 61 years to remember how much she love her, but Fanny insisted on this display.

Grandma Fanny tol' Ceil, as if I wasn't there, how she loved settin' with her on the porch swing every night for 41 years an' holdin' her hand. How she loved raisin' my mama with her, how soft her skin used to be 'fore she got old and wrinkly. She chuckled softly, sayin' she liked her old wrinkly skin, too. I listened to 'em talk back an' forth 'bout the special times in they life an' the special private times they shared. I sit in that there room that was gettin' darker an' darker, none of us movin' to light a candle, listenin' with my heart open an' the tears an' laughter comin' at regular spaces.

We got quiet an' I think we mighta dozed a piece an' I hear Grandma Ceil snifflin' a little an' I have a funny feelin' in my stomach. I's wonderin' if'n I'm jest hungry, it bein' so long since dinner. Grandma Ceil whispers, "I love you," and Grandma Fanny must be asleep 'cuz she adds, "Sweet Dreams."

'Course, after realizin' Grandma Fanny had passed on, the followin' weeks was in a blur a' food, family, friends, and neighbors caterin' to my only Grandma left. Durin' the months that Grandma Ceil hurt an' cried, I stayed as often as I could get 'way with without losin' my job. My search for a Fanny a' my own gave way to lovin' an' dotin' a way I never'd done in my whole life.

It seemed too long 'fore Grandma Ceil would leave the house. We'd all been fetchin' for her down the store an' doin' her chores an' all. I came back from Montgomery nigh on fourteen months after Fanny'd passed on. Grandma Ceil looked sadder'n ever and I thought she'd die from no sun on her face for so long. I tol' her she had to get outta the house 'fore she turned to stone. She said she didn't want nothin' to do with nobody 'cept me and Fanny's ghost. I tol' her to ask Grandma Fanny if'n she been sad long enough and if she's able to get on with her life. My Grandma Ceil was madder'n I ever seen her and hollered at me all the way out the porch.

Next time I come, a bit more scared, to see my Grandma, she welcome me in an' ast me how I was. I see she'd got herself some sun, but I didn't dare say nothin' for fear she'd holler me out again. After she'd fed me proper, she ast me if'n I though she was sinful on account a' she was lonely an' wanted company in her house again. I held in my burst a' joy so's not to scare her 'way and tol' her I was right happy for her she wanted a friend. I said since she still feelin' afraid, she might find some peace if'n she walked down to the crik an' healed the last part of her guilty heart. She said she been thinkin' 'bout seein' the crik again of late and, now that I said it was okay, she jest might do go.

Comin' 'round was gettin' to be a regular adventure. I came in an' Grandma Ceil introduced me to Miz Emma. Emma'd moved to this side a' town las' year an' when Grandma went down to the crik like I suggested, she met up with Emma, a spry sixty-seven-year-old. Emma'd been down the crik 'cuz she said it pulled her like a bee to a flower. Grandma Ceil and me, we looked to each other and smiled. Miz Emma, I knowed in my heart, was gonna be my Grandma Emma one day.

She weren't for a long time, but sure 'nough, she were. I often remember how my two grandmas looked and sounded that peaceful day when Grandma Fanny passed on. I tell my Phoebe 'bout it prob'ly more'n she can stand to hear it tell. My Grandma Ceil, Grandma Fanny, and Grandma Emma done taught me more'n they ever knowed. An' I love 'em all for it, more'n I can ever say.

Barbara Herrera is a woman who loves women. A Cuban-American, she has three children—a son born in the hospital, a daughter born at home, and a daughter born in the car. As a birth assistant for Latina and poor women, she strives to make the transition into motherhood a more natural and gentle one. A writer since childhood, she encourages everyone to tell their story.

PARADIGM
Publishing Company

Paradigm Publishing Company, a women owned press, was founded to publish works created within communities of diversity. These communities are empowering themselves and society by the creation of new paradigms which are inclusive of diversity. We are here to raise their voices.

Books Published by Paradigm Publishing:

Taken By Storm by Linda Kay Silva
(Lesbian Fiction/Mystery)
A Delta Stevens police action novel, intertwining mystery, love, and personal insight. The first in a series. ISBN 0-9628595-1-6 $8.95
". . . not to be missed!" — East Bay Alternative

Expenses by Penny S. Lorio (Lesbian Fiction/Romance)
A novel that deals with the cost of living and the price of loving. ISBN 0-9628595-0-8 $8.95
"I laughed, I cried, I wanted more!" — Marie Kuda, Gay Chicago Magazine

Tory's Tuesday by Linda Kay Silva (Lesbian Fiction)
Linda Kay Silva's second novel is set in Bialystok, Poland during 1939 Nazi occupation. Marissa, a Pole, and Elsa, a Jew, are two lovers who struggle not only to stay together, but to stay alive in Auschwitz concentration camp during the horrors of World War II. ISBN 0-9628595-3-2 $8.95
"*Tory's Tuesday* is a book that should be widely read — with tissues close at hand — and long remembered." — Andrea L.T. Peterson, The Washington Blade

Practicing Eternity by Carol Givens and L. Diane Fortier (Nonfiction/Healing/Lesbian and Women's Studies)
The powerful, moving testament of partners in a long-term lesbian relationship in the face of Carol's diagnosis with cervical cancer. ISBN 0-9628595-2-4 $10.05
"*Practicing Eternity* is one of the most personal and moving stories

I have read in years." —Margaret Wheat, We The People

Seasons of Erotic Love by Barbara Herrera (Lesbian Erotica)
A soft and sensual collection of lesbian erotica with a social conscience that leaves us empowered with the diversity in the lesbian community. ISBN 0-9628595-4-0 $8.95

Evidence of the Outer World by Janet Bohac (Women's Short Stories)
Janet Bohac, whose writing has appeared in various literary publications, brings us a powerful collection of feminist and women centered fiction. ISBN 0-9628595-5-9 $8.95

The Dyke Detector (How to Tell the Real Lesbians from Ordinary People) by Shelly Roberts/Illustrated by Yani Batteau
The Dyke Detector is lesbian humor at its finest: poking fun at our most intimate patterns and outrageous stereotypes. This is side-splitting fun from syndicated columnist Shelly Roberts. ISBN 0-9628595-6-7 $7.95
"What a riot! A must read for all lesbians. Brilliant!" — JoAnn Loulan

Paradigm Publishing Ordering Information

Our books are available through your local bookstore.

Or if you wish to **mail order direct** with us:

Please provide us with a **list of the titles** you wish to order with the amount of each book. **California residents add appropriate sales tax.**

Postage and Handling—
Domestic Orders: $2.00 for the first book and $.50 for each additional book. Foreign Orders: $2.50 for the first book and $1.00 for each additional book (surface mail).

Make **check or money order**, in U.S. currency, payable **to:** Paradigm Publishing, P.O. Box 3877, San Diego, CA 92163

Provide us with **your name, address including zip code, and phone number including area code.** This is the address to which you want the books shipped.

Bookstores and quantity orders, please contact Paradigm Publishing at (619)234-7115 for our discount schedule or order through Inland, Bookpeople, bookslinger, or New Leaf distributors.

Thank you for your support of Paradigm Publishing Company.